LITTLE PROFESSOR SKYE
Favorite Things

Written by Munson Steed
Illustrated by Kareem Kenyada

Reading is one of my favorite things to do!

STEED PUBLISHING

Copyright © 2016 by Steed Publishing

ISBN: 978-0-9964293-3-7

10 9 8 7 6 5 4 3 2   0 3 1 8 1 6

Printed in the United States of America

∞ This paper meets the requirements of ANSI/NISO Z39.48-1992 (Permanence of Paper)

Illustrator: Kareem Kenyada
Photo Credit: Dewayne Rogers

Name:

Age:

Favorite
things:

Dream. Simply dream. That is all I want you to do as you read and enjoy the Little Professor Skye series. Each time you read a book, it should awaken your imagination to create possibility. Reading encourages you to experience new ideas and new adventures. Get inspired to share and create as a family.

3

One of my favorite things is dreaming. I love dreaming because Daddy says the best dreams can come true.

13

You have such beautiful teeth. I can see you brush your teeth often.

I squeeze toothpaste on my toothbrush and begin to brush those germs away. My smile is so bright. I cannot wait to show everyone my smile today.

Next, I wash my face to make sure my skin is clean and clear. Brushing my teeth and washing my face are two of my favorite things.
Great! These are two of my favorite things now, too!

Wow! The Magic Closet has attire for every occasion.

Daddy says I must dress for success. The Magic Closet makes it possible to go wherever I dream, but only if I choose to wear the right thing.

In the Magic Closet, we can use our imagination to go everywhere and do everything we dream!

I love to play soccer with my friends.
I bump the ball with my head and kick
it with my feet. What a treat! I practice
karate because I love the discipline of
the sport and I also love to compete.
I love ballet. I am a ballerina in my heart.
One day, I will compete in the Olympics
because I love to swim. These are my
favorite things, and what I wear when
I'm doing each of them.

Give someone flowers to show how much you care. Care to share the love of flowers when one is in despair. Flowers will brighten anyone's day, even when skies are gray. Flowers are a gift of smiles, and smiles will dry the rain away. Helping people to be happy is my favorite occupation. I would love to bring you flowers for your favorite situation.

I love to play music on various instruments. I compose songs for my friends and perform for my family. I am multitalented.
Each day, I practice and become better at creating beautiful music. Practice is one of my favorite things because then I can create one of your favorite songs.

Whether you like to travel to other worlds, define some other words, or find a recipe, you can find it in a book. Find a jazz musician you have heard, there are so many different types of birds, everything is hidden in a book. Libraries are my favorite places to look.

Libraries have helpers who help you get things done. These helpers are called librarians. Librarians make doing research fun.

Doing homework is a breeze because librarians know their way around. Librarians are some of my favorite people who love to help us check out our favorite books.

CHECK OUT BOOKS HERE

I love reading. But I also love writing. Sometimes I am so inspired, I write letters to all of my favorite people.

US MAIL
Little Professor Skye, I see you are still writing letters to everyone.
Writing letters is my favorite thing to do. I give all my letters to you when I'm done.
Postal workers are special people who take care of all the letters that we send. They carry our letters to our favorite people. We wouldn't have deliveries without them.
US MAIL
MAIL
Skye

I wrote a letter to U.S. President Barack Obama
and his wife, Michelle, the first lady. I shared that
I admire them and they are two of my favorite people.
They received my letter and decided to visit my school.
They read a book to my class. It was my favorite day.

One day, my class went to the Museum of Natural History. Museums are big and wonderful. They preserve our history and give us plenty of new things to learn.

We had fun at the museum because we got to see the exhibits and meet many scientists, researchers and historians who know so much about the world.

Little Professor Skye probably does not know how much it means to me to see Skye and the Highlights sing in the talent show. The music is really cool and they make me want to dance. I love to go to their talent shows whenever I have a chance. Skye and the Highlights are so cool. They are the rockstars of their school. You would love to hear them sing. It will be one of your favorite things.

There is trouble at the table. Label me unable to resist the tangerines, strawberries, and chocolate twists. We love our princess parties. We love to celebrate. We share with everybody. We all participate. Princesses grant your favorite wishes and serve your favorite dishes. We talk about our favorite toys that we would want our parents to get us. Dance to our favorite songs. We can stay up late, so let us get down to business. Tell all of your friends. We would love to have them visit.

48

Scary story time is more than I can bear. In my tale, I am walking in the dark forest and I meet a witch with a curdling stare. The next time I go, I will take all of my favorite things to keep me safe while I'm there.

Today was my favorite day because I got to spend it with you.
Today was my favorite day because I learned all of your favorite things. There was so much to see, so much to explore. Tomorrow, I hope there will be more.

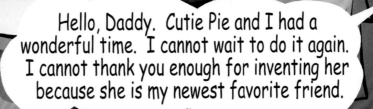

53

About the Author

A graduate of Morehouse College, **Munson Steed** is a prominent entrepreneur, motivational speaker, artist and thought provoker. As CEO of Steed Media Group, Inc., Munson has steered his publication, **RollingOut** into national prominence as the largest African-American weekly paper in the nation.

Inspired by the interest of his seven-year-old Goddaughter, **Skye Johnson**, Munson is now introducing the Little Professor Skye series to open the imaginations of young readers.

Journal

Journal